For Marc, Adriel, and Yuna.
— Susanna Isern

For Yago, who gets my mail, wherever he is.
— Daniel Montero Galán

The Lonely Mailman
Text © 2016 Susanna Isern
Illustrations © 2016 Daniel Montero Galán
This edition © 2016 Cuento de Luz SL
Calle Claveles, 10 | Urb. Monteclaro | Pozuelo de Alarcón | 28223 | Madrid | Spain
www.cuentodeluz.com
Title in Spanish: Cartas en el bosque
English translation by Jon Brokenbrow
ISBN: 978-84-16147-98-4
3nd printing
Printed in PRC by Shanghai Chenxi Printing Co., Ltd. August 2017, print number 1617-9

THE LONELY MAILMAN

Susanna Isern

Daniel Montero Galán

Every morning, just as the sun is rising, the old mailman leaves his house with a bag full of letters. He climbs onto his bicycle, and sets off on his way.

The mailman goes to each door, rings the bell, and only says four words:

"Squirrel! Letter for you!"

He whispers so quietly that even he can hardly hear the words.

"Hedgehog! Letter for you!"

```
Dear Squirrel,
Sorry about pricking you yesterday
when I bumped into you at the market.
To make up for it, come over for dinner
at eight, and don't be late!
        —Hedgehog
```

Dear Hedgehog,

I know you pricked me yesterday, but don't worry, I know you didn't mean to! If you invite me for dinner, we can have a chat. I'll be there at eight, so see you then.

—Squirrel

Sometimes, the animals that live in the forest offer him a cup of coffee. But the mailman always smiles, says, "No thank you," and rides off in a cloud of dust.

"Dormouse! Letter for you!"

Sorry Dormouse,
I only realized yesterday that I'm tapping away next to your nest. I know how much you like to rest, so I'm off to find another tree to peck.

—Woodpecker

He never gets off his bicycle.

"Woodpecker! Letter for you!"

Dear Woodpecker,
The tree where you started to peck
is next to my nest, and now I can
hardly sleep! Couldn't you move to
another tree?

    —Dormouse

The animals see him cycling through the forest every day. But they hardly know him.

"Butterfly! Letter for you!"

In fact, nobody knows anything about the mailman at all.

"Turtle! Letter for you!"

```
Beautiful Butterflies,
There's plenty of room on my shell,
where you can sunbathe in peace and
quiet. And if it starts to rain, you can
all come inside for a cup of tea.
        —Turtle
```

Dear Wise Old Turtle,
We'd love to come and visit you, to flutter
around and keep you cool, and sit a while on
your lovely shell, listening to your tales
while we enjoy the sun.
    —The Butterflies

Some of the animals think that the mailman is sad, and that's why he doesn't say much.

"Bear! Letter for you!"

But nobody really knows, because nobody's ever asked him.

"Rabbit! Letter for you!"

Dear Bear,
When I see you swimming in the lake, I want to be there with you. But I feel a bit scared, because I am afraid to get water in my ears and I can't swim.
—Rabbit

Dear Rabbit,
I've had a great idea for when I'm bathing in the lake. You can climb up on my back, just as if I were a big old boat.
—Bear

All through the day, the old mailman rides around delivering mail in the forest. He visits the wolf, the deer, the frogs, the beaver, the fox, the skunk, and the fish in the river.

At last the sun sets,
and the mailman
has no more letters
in his bag.

Feeling very tired,
he heads home.

Every night, the old mailman sits down in the flickering candlelight and writes letters. They are the letters he'll be delivering the next day: invitations, apologies, plans, and messages full of love.

He writes and writes until he's exhausted, then falls fast asleep on top of his typewriter.

One day, when the mailman is just about to finish his round, something amazing happens. The last letter has his name and his address written on the envelope.

It's a letter for him!

The mailman nervously heads home.
It's the first time he's ever had a letter.
When he arrives, he puts it in the
mailbox, and whispers four words:

"Mailman! Letter for you!"

Then he opens the mailbox, takes out
the letter, and enters his house.

Dear Mailman,
For a long time, your letters have
filled our days with love and
happiness. But now we've discovered
your secret, and we want to thank you.
Most of all, we want to share
our happiness with you.

　　　—The Forest Animals

The old mailman feels a big lump in his throat, and his eyes fill with tears.

Suddenly, the old doorbell lets out a rusty squeak. It is the first time anyone has ever come to the mailman's door.

He plucks up his courage, and opens the door. Outside, the forest animals are waiting. When they see him, they all rush over.

The old mailman smiles and blushes amongst all the cheers and hugs. And then he begins to think about all the letters he'll be writing tonight . . .